PHILIP
FROM DEA
TO EVANGE

The Called Out Ones Series

Ashley Adams

PHILIP, FROM DEACON TO EVANGELIST

Printed in the United States of America

BOOK COVER DESIGNED BY GERMAN CREATIVE

DEDICATION

This book is dedicated to all the servants of the Lord Jesus, who tirelessly spread His Gospel and unselfishly spread His love. May God continue to use, bless, and cover you.

SPECIAL THANK YOU TO MY MOTHER STELLA ADAMS AND MY LEADERS

Apostles Christopher and DeShanna Collins
As well as my family and friends.

TABLE OF CONTENTS

INTRODUCTION

Jesus Christ had met with the Apostles for the last time before ascending to the throne with God, and He left the Apostles with some instructions. Now was the time to receive the comforter and advocate of God, the "Holy Spirit." Jesus told the Apostles, "*I must go, so he "Holy Spirit" can come* (John 16:7)." The day of Pentecost was the landmark of the receiving of the Holy Spirit, but also a new movement had been birthed, and "whosoever" was in activation in John 3:16. Jesus came to His own and they received Him not (John 1:11). Now was the time where salvation was offered up to the Gentiles. In Acts 2:40-47, God was adding to the church daily; not monthly or yearly. The church was growing at a rapid rate and with this growth, problems arose.

There has to be a reason for why you do what you do. Many are in the church/ministry without knowing why they are there or knowing what God said or requires. See, there was a need for Philip and the other men. They did not promote themselves. They were called by God and chosen by man through the finger of God. You are here for a reason. Seek God to find out why.

The Gospel of Jesus Christ was now being spread, and that was good news. Many new converts were selling their property and possession and giving them to the Apostles. What a movement! A new, fresh thing. However, with the new era came problems in the church!!!

THE TIMES OF THE GENTILES

"To everything there is a season, and a time to every purpose under the heaven:"
Ecclesiastes 3:1

Many scholars believe the times of the Gentiles occurred during the reign of Nebuchadnezzar. The exact date of the time is not the concern, but the events indicating it, I will be pointing out to you. If you have read the Old Testament, one would see how God adopted Gentiles into His nation called Israel. I will give you two people who were classified as "Gentiles," but God allowed them to be listed in the genealogy of Christ in Matthew 1. The two individuals are Rahab and Ruth. See, God always had a redemption plan for His people. It started out as a certain group who he claimed out of the seed of Abraham and used through Jacob/Israel. Now under this new covenant through Jesus Christ, any person that believes in Jesus will be saved (John 3:16). God knew the time was coming when Israel would rebel, which allowed God to look for another people. There is still hope for Israel and for a limited time hope for the Gentiles as well.

"The Lord is not slack concerning his promise, as some men count slackness; but is longsuffering to us-ward, not willing that any should perish, but that all should come to repentance."
2 Peter 3:9

GREAT MYSTERY

The great mystery that God revealed in the New Testament through the Apostle Paul comes from Ephesians 3:3-6 (Amplified Classic Edition Version), *"And that the mystery (secret) was made known to me and I was allowed to comprehend it by direct revelation, as I already briefly wrote you.when you read this you can understand my insight into the mystery of Christ. {This mystery) was never disclosed to human beings in past generation as it has now been revealed to His holy apostles (consecrated messengers) and prophets by the (Holy) Spirit. (It is this) that the Gentiles are now to be fellow heirs (with the Jews), members of the same body and joint partakers (sharing) in the same divine promise in Christ through (their acceptance of) the glad tidings (the Gospel)."*

Jesus stated in the Bible, ***"I came to my own and they received me not," John 1:11.*** The nation of Israel refused Jesus as their savior, which allowed the Gentiles an opportunity for salvation. In Romans 11:11, it stated, ***through Israel's fall salvation is come unto the Gentiles.*** This same chapter showed us the current state of the Israelites proving that blindness was upon them.

> *"For I would not, brethren, that ye should be ignorant of this mystery, lest ye should be wise in your own conceits; that blindness in part is happened to Israel, until the fullness of the Gentiles be come in."*
> ***Romans 11: 25***

We are currently in the times of the Gentiles. This is just not the time where the Gentile nations rule, but also for salvation to come to the Gentiles as well. The Lord and His prophets warn Israel that their disobedience and idol worship would bring sudden destruction upon themselves. In Nehemiah 1:8, *"Remember, I beseech thee, the word that thou commandedest thy servant Moses, saying, if ye transgress, I will scatter you abroad among the nations."* In Israel's disbelief and rebellion, it allowed salvation to Gentiles. The Apostle Paul warns the Gentiles by telling them *if God did not spare the natural branches (Israel), take heed lest he also spare not thee* (Romans 11:21).

THERE IS HOPE FOR ISRAEL!

"And so, all Israel shall be saved; as it is written, there shall come out of Sion the Deliver and shall turn away ungodliness from Jacob:"
Romans 11:26

At the end of the times for the Gentiles, God will shift His focus directly on the Israelites- God's chosen people. The children of Israel are scattered throughout this world. They are not currently in one location but still scattered (Ezekiel 36:19). For those that are in doubt and believe that Israel was united in the New Testament, James 1:1, he stated: *"to the twelve tribes which are scattered abroad."* God makes promises to gather the nation of Israel back together and their land (Ezekiel 11:17).

WHO IS ISRAEL?

God made a covenant with Abraham that he would cause many descendants to come from him, the father of many nations (Genesis 17:1-6). Abraham had a son named Isaac (Genesis 21), and Isaac had a son named Jacob, whose name changed to Israel (Genesis 25:24-26). God also made a covenant with Israel in Deuteronomy 29, where the ***"Hebrews"*** would be His people, and He would be their only God. Israel has 12 tribes which are named after Jacob; Abraham's grandson, Genesis 32:24-26. God chose 12 sons from Jacob whose name was changed to Israel. The 12 tribes/sons are listed in Deuteronomy 33 and Genesis 49:1-33:

12 TRIBES OF ISRAEL

Manasseh	Reuben	Simeon
Judah	Zebulun	Issachar
Dan	Gad	Asher
Naphtali	Joseph	Benjamin

The tribes of Dan and Ephraim were replaced, and the Tribes of Levi and Joseph were included in the book of Revelation 7:5-8. In Judges 18:30-31, it recalls the behavior and demeanor of the tribe of Dan as idol worshippers. However, the tribe of Dan is listed in Ezekiel 48:1-3.

GENTILE RULES

By this time, one should see that Israel is split into 2 kingdoms: Northern and the Southern. I want to talk about when Judah, the Southern kingdom, was seized by King Nebuchadnezzar. God used His prophets to warn the people of coming destructions. Also, there were many false prophets who came to counteract against God's words. The Southern tribes did just as their sister tribes did, who were rebels who disobeyed God's commandments. In Ezekiel 21:1-27, a prophet named Ezekiel warns the people that God has given the king of Babylon permission to seize us. See, Israel as a whole desired to worship other gods besides the true living God. Being God's chosen people was not enough for Israel, and thus, they wanted more.

"For thou shalt worship no other god: for the LORD, whose name is Jealous, is a jealous God:"
Exodus 34:14

The Gentile nation came into rule because Israel sinned against God and the acts of "whoredom" with other pagan gods. Israel was God's possession, and He was jealous of her. Israel was deemed by God as unfaithful, and God gave Israel exactly want she wanted, and that was to be like the other nations without a true living God.

"And I, when for all the causes whereby backsliding Israel committed adultery I had put her away, and given her a bill of divorce; yet her treacherous sister Judah feared not, but went and played the harlot also."
Jeremiah 3:8

GREAT DIVORCE OF UNITED ISRAEL

The 12 Tribes that were listed previously are split into 2 kingdoms: Northern and the Southern Kingdoms. Below are the tribes split between these kingdoms.

12 TRIBES

NORTHERN

- Asher
- Simon
- Dan
- Naphtali
- Zebulun
- Manasseh
- Ephraim
- Reuben
- Gad
- Issachar

SOUTHERN

- Judah
- Benjamin

In Revelation 7:7-8 the tribes of Levi and Joseph are included, and the tribes Dan and Ephraim is not mention!

After Solomon's death, his son Rehoboam was set to become the next king. Jeroboam returned from Egypt and led a group of people to confront Rehoboam with a mandate for a lighter tax burden. The elders warned Rehoboam of the senseless tax and the burden he has put on Israel. When Rehoboam refused the demand, ten of the tribes rejected Rehoboam and David's lineage (1 Kings 12:16), and Ahijah's prophecy was fulfilled. Only Judah and Benjamin remained loyal to King Rehoboam. The northern tribes crowned Jeroboam as their king. Rehoboam made plans to mount an assault on the rebel tribes, but the Lord prevented him from taking that action (1 Kings 12: 21-24). Meanwhile, Jeroboam further joined his power by starting a form of pagan "calf" worship distinctive to his kingdom and declaring that, changed the place of worship instead of it originally being Jerusalem. Thus, the people of the northern tribes would have no communication with the tribes of Judah and Benjamin.

"Therefore the Lord was very angry with Israel, and removed them out of his sight: there was none left but the tribe of Judah only."
2 Kings 17:18

"So Israel "Ephraim" has been in rebellion against the house of David to this day."
1 Kings 12:19

Israel/Ephraim "The Northern Kingdom" (10 tribes) were the first to go into exile under Assyrian rule (2 Kings 17). It was many years later before Judah would fall under Babylonian Rule (Jeremiah 28). Judah was just as wicked and evil as her sister "Israel" and was seized by King Nebuchadnezzar. Jeremiah, the prophet, warns the Southern tribes of destructions that were coming. He stated that a man named King Nebuchadnezzar was sent by God to bring the southern tribes into exile in Babylon.

"Therefore thus says the Lord of hosts: Because you have not obeyed my words, I am going to send for all the tribes of the north, says the Lord, even for King Nebuchadnezzar of Babylon, my servant, and I will bring them against this land and its inhabitants, and against all these nations around; I will utterly destroy them, and make them an object of horror and of hissing, and an everlasting disgrace."
Jeremiah 25:8-9 NRSV

"After that, declares the LORD, I will hand over King Zedekiah of Judah, his officers, and the people in this city who survive the plague and sword and famine, to King Nebuchadnezzar of Babylon and to their enemies who seek their lives. He will put them to the sword; he will not spare them or show pity or compassion."
Jeremiah 21:7 NLT

The Bible stated that Israel and Judah will connect and be reunited again.

"And he shall set up an ensign for the nations, and shall assemble the outcasts of Israel, and gather together the dispersed of Judah from the four corners of the earth. The envy also of Ephraim shall depart, and the adversaries of udah shall be cut off: Ephraim shall not envy Judah, and Judah shall not vex Ephraim."
Isaiah 11:12-13

BABYLON

Now both kingdoms of Israel are in captivity. The Northern kingdom was the first to go under the Assyrian rule and then the Southern kingdom under Babylon. In Daniel 2, King Nebuchadnezzar had a disturbing dream that when he woke up, he forgot all about it. He called his court in to help him remember the dream as well as interpret it. But not one on the king's staff was able to help him. That made Nebuchadnezzar angry, and he sent out a decree to kill all the wise men.

"For this cause the king was angry and very furious, and commanded to destroy all the wise men of Babylon."
Daniel 2:12

The decree the king sent out was harsh. However, it had to be sent out that way for the chosen servant of God, *"Daniel,"* Babylonian name *"Belteshazzar"* to be used by God. In that chapter of Daniel, the king's court told the king that what he requires of them is a task that can only be done by ***"gods that does not dwell in flesh"*** (Daniel 2:11). Daniel was that godman who chose not to defile himself even as a slave in exile. Daniel decided to be different and not conform to the pagan culture (Daniel 1:12-16). God had given Daniel understanding in all visions and dreams (v. 17). Daniel was qualified but was not in a position to be used until now. When we read further in the chapter, we see that Daniel reveals the dream to the king and explained it also. The statue the king dreamed of still affects us to this day.

Example of the statue King Nebuchadnezzar dreamed of...

Copy right @ https://goodnewsshared.wordpress.com

We are in the kingdom of the clay and Iron; The Roman empire fell under Barbarian invasion ____ancient.eu/article/835/fall-of-the-western-roman-empire/.

Times of Gentile Rule
Daniel 2

GOLD – BABYLON

SILVER – MEDO PERSIAN

BRONZE – GREECE

IRON – ROME

IRON AND CLAY – ROME AND DIVIDED KINGDOMS

We are in the kingdom of the clay and Iron; The Roman empire fell under Barbarian invasion ____ancient.eu/article/835/fall-of-the-western-roman-empire/.

United Rome is no longer the superpower in the world. One must understand Babylon, Medo-Persia, Greece and Rome ruled as the only superpower in the whole world. Now, we have many superpowers in the world. We have a diverse mixture of superpowers, which explains the last kingdom being mixed with the Roman Empire but also a mixture of another substance, "clay." The last empire will still have a connection, and some appearance of Rome due to what the Bible says "Iron- Rome mixing with clay." Many scholars believe this mixture is political as well as religious, pointing to a certain denomination and group of people.

Since Israel went into exile, the Gentiles have been in rule due to their punishment that God stated would come as a result of Israel's disobedience. Israel's first mistake was wanting to be like their enemies. They asked the prophet, Samuel, to give them a king like the other nations. See, God was Israel's king, and He made Israel's name well known among her enemies. However, that was not good enough for Israel. The prophet Samuel was getting old, and his sons did not walk in the ways of God. The people got together and decided now is the time to have a king to rule over us. One may not view what Israel asked for as wrong for wanting a king, and besides, Samuel's sons were not fit to rule over them. The problem was Israel wanted a king like their defeated enemies. The meeting with the prophet Samuel could have been totally different. For instance, saying, Samuel, your sons, are wicked and don't' walk in the ways of God. Ask God to get us a king after His heart. It was like they could not trust the God who had given them many victories to give them a king after His heart.

"Then all the elders of Israel gathered themselves together, and came to Samuel unto Ramah, And said unto him, Behold, thou art old, and thy sons walk not in thy ways: now make us a king to judge us like all the nations. But the thing displeased Samuel, when they said, give us a king to judge us. And Samuel prayed unto the Lord."
1 Samuel 8:4-6

God told Samuel to give the people what they ask for. The prophet Samuel warned Israel of what their very own king would do. You can read from 1 Samuel 8:10-22 of the mannerism this particular king would have. The king that Israel requested would make the people of Israel slaves. Israel's request was basically putting them back into bondage again.

"And you yourselves will become slaves of this king. When that time comes, you will cry because of the king you chose. But the Lord won't answer you at that time. But the people would not listen to Samuel. They said, "No, we want a king to rule over us. Then we will be the same as all the other nations. Our king will lead us. He will go before us and fight our battles."

1 Samuel 8:17-19 Easy to Read Version

Samuel listened to the people and then repeated their words to the Lord. The Lord answered, "Listen to them and give them a king.

Then Samuel told the Israelites, "You will have a king. Now go home."

1 Samuel 8: 17b-22

The Gentile Kingdom ruling over Israel was destined to come due to their sinful desires and pagan acts. God continues to warn Israel of their sinful acts and punishments. However, Israel refused to listen to God.

"If my people, which are called by my name, shall humble themselves, and pray, and seek my face, and turn from their wicked ways; then will I hear from heaven, and will forgive their sin, and will heal their land."

2 Chronicles 7:14

"My people are destroyed for lack of knowledge: because thou hast rejected knowledge, I will also reject thee, that thou shalt be no priest to me: seeing thou hast forgotten the law of thy God, I will also forget thy children."

Hosea 4:6

"Therefore, my people will go into exile for their lack of understanding; their dignitaries are starving, and their masses are parched with thirst."

Isaiah 5:13

Israel becoming slaves to the Gentile nation had already started with their own kings in place. Even in the time of Philip until today, the Gentile nation is still in rule until God stops it. In the times of Philip, United Rome was ruling as the only superpower. The church was growing but under an attack. It reminds me of the scenario in Exodus, when Pharaoh wanted the Hebrews' newborns killed and, miraculously, the Hebrew population increased.

"There were two Hebrew[a] nurses who helped the Israelite women give birth. They were named Shiphrah and Puah. The king of Egypt said to the nurses, "You will continue to help the Hebrew women give birth to their children. If a girl baby is born, let the baby live. But if the baby is a boy, you must kill him! The nurses trusted God, so he was good to them and allowed them to have their own families. The Hebrews continued to have more children, and they became very strong. So Pharaoh gave this command to his own people: "If the Hebrew women give birth to a baby girl, let it live. But if they have a baby boy, you must throw it into the Nile River."

Exodus 1:15-16;20-22
Easy to Read Version

The decree to murder stimulated the census of God's people. Though it does not make sense, it still happened. In the days of Philip, an attack against the people of God, the believers of Christ Jesus were initiated. Many were murdered and suffered for the sake of Jesus's name, but the church and body of Christ grew.

We are currently at the parts of the toes, iron mixed with miry clay. The scripture explained that the two cannot properly mix. They are joined, but not connected. What does the iron signify? The Roman Empire, which is the last kingdom that ruled the whole world. They will mix with the seed of men.

CHURCH AGE

Let me paint the scene for you! Jesus Christ has just been crucified, buried, and risen after the third day. Now let's visit the Book of Acts where the Apostles who followed Jesus are in the upper room waiting by commands of their master for the promise from God, "of the Holy Spirit" (Acts 1) and Judas, who betrayed Jesus, is replaced by Matthias (Acts 1:26). On the day on Pentecost, the Bible stated in Acts 2:1, "*They were all with one accord in one place,*" It was important for the disciples of Jesus, now Apostles, to receive the Holy Spirit because Jesus had asked for an advocate from God to help them (John 14:15-17), and also He was going to lead and guide them into all truth (John 16:13). The Holy Spirit is mandatory; without it, one does not belong to God (Romans 8:9). Therefore, the Apostles and the others in the upper room were filled with the Holy Spirit and equipped to do great works of God. Now we have embarked on the salvation and times for the Gentiles.

The times of the Gentiles were foretold "prophesied" in the book of Luke 21:24, *"And they shall fall by the edge of the sword, and shall be led away captive into all nations: and Jerusalem shall be trodden down of the Gentiles, until the times of the Gentiles be fulfilled."*

PHILIP – THE DEACON

"And in those days, when the number of the disciples was multiplied, there arose a murmuring of the Grecians against the Hebrews, because their widows were neglected in the daily ministration."
Acts 6:1

Hellenists felt their widows were being neglected, and the Hebrew widows were not. The Apostles stated they did not have time to handle this problem and designated the disciples to appoint seven men with certain characteristics to manage this affair. The Apostles recognized the problem and delegated the solution to the disciples. The disciples were told to pick seven men from among them to handle the problem regarding the widows in the church. The seven men had to be full of the Holy Spirit, of good reputation and wisdom.

The seven men included: Stephen, Philip, Prochorus, Nicanor, Timon, Parmenas, Nicolas. The Apostles prayed for these 7 men and laid hands on them. Philip went from an average churchgoer to a leader unexpectedly. He had the qualification because God put it in him. He did not have to make a scene. God already had an appointed time for Philip to come forth to serve the people. Now was the time for Philip to get some training by serving in the church and learning love lessons with diverse people. Philip had no idea what he agreed to do was going to prepare him for the great outdoors.

The Start of Preparation

Immediately Philip started serving in the church. He was no longer just a disciple but now serving, ministering according to studies. Philip became a deacon, he who handled the affairs in the church. He was working alongside six other men.

Philip's job was to make sure that the widows were taken care of, and no one was overlooked. Remember, the church was growing, and the Apostles were busy in the word of God. Philip's job was no walk in the park. He was dealing with diverse cultures as well as the stress of a growing church. Philip had to make sure that the needs of the selected ones were met for a megachurch that was growing daily.

Can one imagine the stress, time, and agitation that went with meeting someone's needs? There were good days as well as bad days, but he had a commission at that moment, and he fulfilled it. Serving in the church prepared Philip for serving in the world. The church was the training grounds. Listen, we get mad with the little number of people we have to deal with daily; imagine the apostles' job. Philip was in the division of customer service. He was dealing with:

- New converts from Gentile nations
- Religious folks
- Time management- there were only seven men dealing with a massive amount of people
- Dealing with needs of individuals

Philip had to learn how to serve with integrity and grace while dealing with people. Philip was being tested in many areas; one can only imagine. Philip was being tested on his:

- Patience- waiting on people, young and old
- Attitudes
- Environment
- Beliefs
- Daily crisis and pressure

All these and more were preparing Philip for something greater than what he could imagine. Philip was going to be used in a great capacity for the kingdom of God. Can I ask you a question? What is God telling you to do? Are you embracing your current position or complaining? Philip could have easily refused the offer of being chosen to serve, but he did not. What is God calling you to do right now? Are you willing to do it? Would your actions right now affect your later?

Power of Love

God chose Philip to work inside the church first, handing the affairs of the church. This was a good practice for Philip, not to mention that his next assignment was outside the church. What can one learn while serving in the church? One significant lesson is how to love people. Love is a major component that is missing in our world and some churches. 1 Corinthians 13 talks about love "charity." I want to point out in 1 Corinthians 13 the actions and reaction without love "charity:"

- A person can speak in heavenly languages, but without love it equals noise.
- You can have faith, gift of understanding and Knowledge; however, if love is not included, it means nothing.
- You can be a great giver and render your body to be burned, but without love, it profits nothing.

See, when you are doing everything without the essential things God said you need, you are just wasting your time with no returns. There is power in God's love, and it is a necessary factor with the labor of God and life overall.

While Philip was serving, his fellow partner was making a scene, Mr. Stephen, himself. The Bible stated Stephen was ***full of faith and power and did great wonders and signs among the people (Acts 6:8).*** Stephen's boldness and preaching were catching the attention of many, especially the Jews. This man was going to be the fire starter that shifted the church into another dimension.

COMPEL THEM TO COME

One of the seven men that was chosen became a trailblazer for the unexpected. This trailblazer's name was Stephen. Stephen, being filled with power and full of faith, got the attention of many people, including certain groups who would cause his death. These groups were: Libertines, Cyrenians, Alexandrians, and some from Cilicia and Asia. The enemy does not mind gathering up a task force to come against you because you are a threat when you are doing the will of God.

"Jesus has manifested, that He might destroy the works of Satan"
1 John 3:8

These individuals from these groups conspired against Stephen and spread lies about his beliefs and teaching, implying that he was against God and Moses. They were painting Stephen as a man who blasphemed against the Lord. This one man caused a group of people from diverse backgrounds to come together to quiet him. That means Stephen was making a lot of noise. Stephen had to be a threat for a group of people to come together to basically silence him. Of course, these group of people could not do what they wanted to do on their own. They needed a community to help back their perverse and evil plans. They gathered false witnesses and false accusations against Stephen.

When you read the short story of Stephen's life, it is as if God made him just to be that spokesman for the new era that was upon the people. Stephen risked his life to tell others the truth about a loving savior named Jesus. He went against traditions and customs, so individuals had an opportunity to be reconciled back to God through Jesus. He was destined to go before the council to give a detailed summary from Abraham to Christ. Stephen was not your average but was willing and obedient until death to do what was required of him by God. He was full of faith, which means he was able to accomplish impossible tasks and behold miraculous things. He had power from God, which means he had the ability to complete things that a normal person had trouble doing. He was bold, which means he was not ashamed or fearful and counted the cost. He had no problem facing religious, prideful, and hateful people, who so happen was his very own by way of culture, ***"Israelites, "***but was an enemy because of their belief.

Now in Acts 7, Stephen is before the council being interrogated. Stephen responds with a brief summary from the beginning with Abraham; Stephen's story was so offensive that in Acts 7:54, *"when they heard these things, they were cut to the heart, and they gnashed on him with their teeth.*" Stephen had an authentic sound about him that insulted the hearts of those that did not receive Jesus as their Lord. His words were real, and it caused a reaction whether a person agreed or not. It is like God made him to make the community and people around him to respond to his words. He could not be ignored.

It was obvious that they did not want to hear what Stephen had to say. It states in Acts 7:57 what the people did "*put their hands over their ears."* Make him stop! Do you ever get mad when someone says something to you that you disagree with or you hear a sound that annoys you? Well, Stephen was that annoying sound and disagreeable voice! Stephen died at the hands of his accusers and even in death, he asked God not to count his death against them. Wow! Stephen was still considering his enemies, even in death.

PHILIP – THE EVANGELIST

"And Saul was consenting unto his death. And at that time there was a great persecution against the church which was at Jerusalem; and they were all scattered abroad throughout the regions of Judaea and Samaria, except the apostles. And devout men carried Stephen to his burial, and made great lamentation over him. As for Saul, he made havock of the church, entering into every house, and haling men and women committed them to prison."

ACTS 8:1-3

Now the church was under great persecution, and the ringleader was Saul of Taurus. Stephen was just killed, and the word is out, "run for your life." Public enemy # 1 is now the church. Saul was going into every believer of Jesus' house and making them go to prison. People were running for safety. In the meantime, Philip, one of the chosen seven, went to a city called Samaria. It seemed like this was the wrong time to be a believer or a minister of Christ Jesus. While the church was under attack, this great movement was going on. Salvation was being preached to other territories, and people were getting healed and delivered. There is never a good time when it comes to ministry, and it is why we have to always stay on God's timing.

"To everything there is a season, a time for every purpose under heaven."

Ecclesiastes 3:1

God set the schedule, seasons, and time. Now was the time for the Gospel to be spread, as well as the people to move into new territories and among different people. Many probably would have asked God how and why? How are we going to spread the Gospel when our lives are at risk? And why during this time while the church is being attacked? God, this does not make sense or line up, right? God always reminds us in His word to count the cost (Luke 14:28). Many people have made the ministry glamorous and safe. Running a ministry God's way is far from glamourous but risky. Jesus stated in his word:

" Then said Jesus unto his disciples, If any man will come after me, let him deny himself, and take up his cross, and follow me. For whosoever will save his life shall lose it: and whosoever will lose his life for my sake shall find it. For what is a man profited, if he shall gain the whole world, and lose his own soul? Or what shall a man give in exchange for his soul?"
Matthew 16: 24-26

"I can do all things through Christ who strengthens me."
Philippians 4:13

The Adventures of Philip

The first stop on this journey with Philip is a well-known city called Samaria. Now, we know about the appointment Jesus had with a particular woman at a well (John 4). The text stated Jesus had to go through Samaria. Samaria was the place that Jesus had to pass through (John 4), where He met the Samarian woman. A lot of history took place in Samaria. There was a particular group of people who were excluded due to their beliefs and practices. Many scholars stated Samaria was a place where people experience racism or discrimination due to interracial marriages; however, it is bigger than that. Samaria had gotten a bad name for being the capital of the Northern kingdom of Israel and Israel intermingling with pagans.

Omri reigned as king in Israel-Northern kingdom and purchased Samaria and practiced paganism. Then Omri had a son name Ahab and you know the rest with Jezebel. See Samaria was a place of idol worship, but it was established by Israel. Samaria was disliked because of their rebellion and practices against God. That's why Jesus told the Samaritan woman when she stated her fathers worshipped in the mountains and Jews' belief of Jerusalem is the place of worship; He replied to the woman,- *you worship what you do not know; Jews know who they worship (John 4:21-22).* Samaria was still the hot spot where God wanted true restoration and worship to come. Now, it was Philip's time to bring good news to Samaria.

Salvation is offered to Samaria

Acts 8 starts off with chilling times; the church was under attack. Saul, the terrorist, was on a mission to stop this "Jesus gospel movement" by any cost. In Saul's effort to persecute the church, it pushed the believers of Jesus to separate and dwell in new locations. The Bible stated, "T*herefore those who were scattered went everywhere preaching the word" (*Acts 8:4). Now the words were being spread by force; the news was out. The times of sitting in the church or temple hearing preached words were gone. Now, you had to practice what you were taught at the state of your life. It was a desperate time, but also the right time for people to know about Jesus. The city of Samaria was in a position to receive Christ.

"And the multitudes with one accord heeded the things spoken by Philip, hearing and seeing the miracles which he did."

Acts 8:6

Many who were suffering in their bodies and minds were being healed as well as salvation was being offered to the city of Samaria-great joy had come upon them. Paul stated in ***Romans 7:21, "I find then a law, that, when I would do good, evil is present with me."*** In the midst of this great revival and demonstration, a man popped up who was moved by the excitement and revival; this man is Simon, the sorcerer. He was a sorcerer because he used his craft to manipulate and deceived the people. Simon tried to make a great name for himself; he deceived the people so that they believed he was a man of God because of his schemes.

People of God, it is imperative you check your motives when connecting with people and when others want to connect with you. Simon wanted to join this movement for the wrong reason. Simon even got baptized and followed after Philip. When the Apostles heard that Samaria had received the word of God, they sent Peter and John to Samaria to bring the Holy Spirit (Acts 8:14-15). Remember, the Holy Spirit is mandatory. The Apostles (Peter and John) came down to lay hands on the people to receive the Holy Spirit. Simon saw this as an opportunity to get the power these Apostles had. Apostle Peter scolded Simon about his motives of believing that he could purchase God's power. Peter told Simon, may your money perish with you; Simon became scared because his true character was revealed, and judgement came upon him.

Crossing Cultures

"This gospel of the kingdom shall be preached in the whole world as a testimony to all the nations and then the end will be."

Matthew 24:14

"For God so loved the world that he gave his only begotten SON, that whosoever shall believe in him shall not perish but have everlasting life."

John 3:16

The Gospel of Christ Jesus must go into all nations before the return of Christ. The next assignment for Philip was with a man from another culture and background. The angel of the Lord gave Philip instructions to go toward the south of Gaza into the desert. Philip had worked in the church and, in the city, but now he was being led to a hot desert. Philip was crossing geographical location and cultures. God can use you to work with diverse nations and in different locations. Only you can stop you! Now Philip is assigned to go to this hot, isolated location to talk to a man from a pagan culture who so happens to be reading the word of God. What a coincidence! Philip walks upon this Ethiopian eunuch reading certain verses from Isaiah 53:7-8 about how Jesus was led like a sheep to be slaughtered. Philip asked the man if he understood what he was reading. Philip asked the man a simple question, and the man stated, how can I? Unless someone teaches or guides me.

He was oppressed, and he was afflicted, yet he opened not his mouth: he is brought as a lamb to the slaughter, and as a sheep before her shearers is dumb, so he openeth not his mouth. He was taken from prison and from judgment: and who shall declare his generation? for he was cut off out of the land of the living: for the transgression of my people was he stricken."

Isaiah 53:7-8

"How then can they call on the One in whom they have believed? And how can they believe in the One of whom they have not heard? And how shall they preach, except they be sent?"

Romans 10:14-15

Philip was the called out one and was sent to help people to have clarity and the opportunity to receive Jesus. Philip seized the opportunity to preach the Gospel to this man to the point where the eunuch wanted salvation and to be baptized. God used Philip so much that he was found doing the miraculous and going to different places spreading the Gospel. When you are doing the will of God, God got you. What does that mean?

- God will supply all your needs.
- God will be your provision.
- God will protect and cover you.
- God will guide you.

Philip was a witness to the fullness of God operating in his life. We do not know about Philip's wife, but the Bible stated that he did have daughters. Paul, on his journey, went to Philip's house.

"Leaving the next day, we reached Caesarea, and we went to stay at the home of Philip the evangelist, who was one of the Seven. He had four unmarried daughters who prophesied."
Acts 21:9

So eventually, Philip was able to have a family, and one can see his ministry had an impact on his daughters. One must understand God's words will not come back to him void. Philip was a perfect example of God's mercy and lovingkindness. God's mission through this man named Philip was to bring back the people who have been separated by sin into a relationship with God. You are so important that God gave His Son Jesus so that you can be saved and have a relationship with God. He even gave His Spirit, the Holy Spirit, so you would have a personal comforter, teacher, and one that guides you into all truth. If that was not enough, He uses people to help you to find Jesus and to have a relationship with God. God has you in mind. He believes you are worth it.

SALVATION PRAYER

If you want to know about Jesus but do not have a relationship with him, here is your opportunity. Romans 10: 9 states, *"That if you confess with your mouth the Lord Jesus and believe in your heart that God has raised Him from the dead, you will be saved."* It is simply a decision that one makes to be willing to have a relationship with God through Jesus. No matter where you are, you can repeat this simple prayer:

> ***"Lord God, I come to you asking you to forgive me of all my sins. I am confessing that I need a savior and I want Jesus to be my Lord and savior. Lord Jesus, come into my heart and life. I believe you have lived and died and risen on the third day. I need you, Lord Jesus. Come in and teach me your way, in Jesus' name. Amen"***

There are many simple prayers you can pray that can bring on salvation, but the above prayer is sufficient. Remember, do not stop there; connect with family or friends who have a relationship with Jesus as well as an organization or church to learn more about Jesus. The Holy Spirit is mandatory, so take a bold step and get baptized. I even got baptized twice, once as a kid, but I did not understand what it was. When I was taught what baptism was, I got baptized again, this time with understanding. You are not alone. If you prayed the salvation prayer and accepted Jesus as your Lord and Savior, you have joined a heavenly kingdom family that belongs to God.

BIBLIOGRAPHY

Ancient History Encyclopedia, 2018

Salt and LightThe Destruction of the Temple and Signs of the End Times, 2017

Bible Gateway, 2020

ABOUT THE AUTHOR

Ashley Adams is a Social Worker, Minister, and Revolutionist with a tremendous experience that helps protect vulnerable populaton and support families in need of assistance. She enjoys nature, research, traveling, and walking. Ashley enjoys baking bread such as banana nut, pumpkin, figs, sweet potato, and jellies in her leisure time. She also loves to write poetry, songs, and mysteries.

Ashley is the founder of "Love Abounds in the Name of Christ." She believes change can occur if one will embrace it. For engagements or connections, feel free to contact her.

You can visit your website at: www.loveabound.org

You can follow her on Facebook and YouTube:
Facebook: love abound in the name of Christ
YouTube: Ashley Adams
Email: ashleyadams@loveabound.org

AVAILABLE BOOKS ON AMAZON
ALSO LOVEABOUND.ORG
BOOKS, CDs, DVDs, T-SHIRTS

Printed in Great Britain
by Amazon

48058902R00020